Proper Dragon Tales No.4

# Muds and Floods

Words and Pictures by Caroline Downey

*Caroline Downey*

The artwork in this book is available as prints.

# This book is dedicated to all those who believe in Dragons

Anyone who has visited the Welsh Black Mountains will know that it is a special place. The relaxed pace of life feels detached from the bustling outside world and even the weather seems to be exclusive to this area.

My fourth Proper Dragon Tale is based on many actual events in the Llanthony Valley and the great storm of September 2008 provided me with plenty of ideas. The Tumble Towers flood is true, my husband and I were having our usual Friday night at the Priory Hotel at the time. On our way home, we towed stranded vehicles from the deep waters on the valley road.

The mention of 'metal monsters' refers to the laying of the National Gas pipeline; its route passes near Hay-on-Wye and around the north side of the Brecon Beacons Mountains.

The 'drowned village' story in Steeply Valley is about the making of the Grwyne Fawr Reservoir – it is said when the water is low you can see the steeple of the church.

'Swim Away Harry' is a real salmon fish that was caught and released again, by Fisherman Jones, into the Usk River. So look out for Harry next time you are walking along the riverbank!

Artist/Author Caroline Downey

# I be the one who tells

My home, in the Black Mountains of Wales, is the best place ever for a dragon to exist. I am kept busy looking over my land spotting all the little creatures – rabbits gather by earthy warrens, while tatty sheep are scattered about in rugged meadows. Ponies graze around the old ruins of Tumble Towers and wait for their time to trek up the mountainsides where sturdy Black Mountain Sheep tread their pathways through the bracken. After centuries of passing, the Crooked Church still clings to the hillside surrounded by the little leaning whitewashed cottages.

I notice the local humble-beings driving along the single valley road, waving and chatting to passing others. They are like a family sharing their lives together, supporting and laughing with their amusing strange talk.

Every time you visit my lovely valley I will know you are here because I see all that happens. While you climb the grassy hills or wade about the ferns and heather on the tops of the mountains, even if you care to explore the dark ancient woods, I will be watching.

Maybe there is a story about you – if you care to listen I might just be the one who tells you a Proper Dragon's Tale. . . . . . . . . . . .

So cwtch up and step into my pages.

# Muds and Floods

After a bitterly cold winter, the dark side of the valley rejoiced when the sunshine returned. As it peeped over the mountain's ridge, the warmth from its brightness tenderly charmed young shoots to sprout early. The meadow grass slowly stretched out their blades, awakening from their long winter's rest. Under the trees, next to the river, wild daffodils pushed through the soil, neatly uncurling their tiny golden trumpets, welcoming the new season.

Sheep, fresh from their lambing sheds, chewed eagerly in the fields, while their new lambs dashed about wagging their woolly tails. Hungry little creatures ventured from their cuddly places, squinting in the new sparkling light, forgetting their deep and endless dreams. Birds sang chirpily, gliding into fluffy clouds and out again under the ceiling of deep blue skies.

Spring had indeed sprung and all was well in my Lovely Valley – but it was only to be a short time later that my dragony ears sensed a curious happening. Heard, when the wind did ease was a faint eerie grunting like an angry monster. As it echoed around the hillsides, the sheep became anxious and baa'd more than usual, looking to the mountains for clues.

All was not as it should be.

There was a happy occasion happening at Golden Glade Warren. The four baby bunnies of Flora and Bobbin hopped excitedly around the clusters of daffodils – it was the day of their naming party.

"Little Ones, come here now!" called Flora their mother, "it's time to give you your proper names." Other rabbits gathered by the hillock waiting for the babies to assemble; some flipped forward their velvety ears to clean, others scratched their scruffs with the long claws of their back paws.

Soon the bunnies were lined up in order of birth while Flora proudly smartened them up by licking the dust from their fur.
"Stop fidgeting Little Ones and listen carefully," she announced proudly. "First we have our eldest – who's quite a handful," the other rabbits laughed in agreement. "I see his wayward spirit causing some tricky times, so we name him Clover for all the extra luck he will need." Bobbin added, "And tomorrow I'll take Clover on his first journey to see Distant Lands."
The others clapped their paws and thumped their back legs on the ground.

Flora smiled and continued. "Our next is a hardy one, so I name him Bramble after a hardy and fruitful plant." Bramble twitched his nose, happy with his name. "Now the one with the big white tail, just like a giant snowflake – he will be called Snowy." Snowy turned and fell over trying to see his amazing tail as he wondered what snow was about.

"Lastly we have our lovely Little One – a sweet pretty thing – she is our Lily of the Valley." Lily gave a toothy grin then hopped away to the riverbank. She peered into the gentle flowing waters of Millydill Pool and in the shade of the trees could see the reflection of her little fluffy face.

"Oh what big eyes I have," and she fluttered her lovely long eyelashes, "and look at my such big teeth – see, no grass stains," talking to herself. Lily wiggled her nose with pride and pondered at her pretty face floating calmly on the river surface, just like a water lily.

Then Lily's furry reflection suddenly rippled and – WHOOSH! Thrusting out of the water emerged some huge slimy lips on a shiny scaly face. "WOW!" she screamed, as she jumped back, startled from the fishy sight.

"It's only me," called Harry Salmon. Lily looked in amazement, "I've never seen a fish like you before!" and was a little scared at the monster fish – but I knew that Harry was a fine and friendly fish from far away.

He explained, "I think I took a wrong turn when finding my way home, I felt so charmed by this beautiful valley, I just couldn't help myself from coming this way," Harry continued with pouted lips, "but now the river is so low I can't swim away." He was indeed trapped in the deep pool of Millydill. Harry turned and dived back down to the Sticklebacks, gently swishing his large tail, waving goodbye to Lily.

The next morning was a fine and sunny day, Bobbin and Clover set off to see Distant Lands. Clover had never gone beyond the shelter of the big trees at Golden Glade and found the open spaces very worrying. Bobbin told him to stay close as they crossed over a meadow of pretty flowers.

In the hedgerow they could hear the chirping of baby birds in their nest and below them was Wodger the Weasel suspiciously snooping about.

Clover had never seen a creature like him before and asked Wodger if he might be a stoat. "A stoat!" cried out Wodger in disgust, "me a silly stoat!" he repeated. "Can't you see I am a weasel?" Bobbin explained that it was Clover's first time out and apologised to Wodger, but Wodger continued instructing Clover. "Listen, a weasel is weaselly recognised and a stoat is stoatally different!" Clover laughed at him, which annoyed Wodger even more and he jumped back into the hedgerow, flicking his tail at them.

Bobbin and Clover squeezed under a wire fence, Clover turned and sniffed it, chewed it, then squeaked with pain as the wire hurt his teeth. Wiping his paw across his mouth they continued until Clover tripped over a molehill. "What on earth is that?" he fretted, then out popped a velvety nose and two flat feet, like pink paddles. "Have you a fat worm for me?" asked Podgy Mole "Sorry," replied Clover timidly. Podgy groaned and wriggled back down to his home to finish nibbling on his old grass roots.

Bobbin and Clover could hear the chugging drone of visiting metal motors; they had come unexpectedly early this spring. Some went slowly with arms pointing out at the landscape, others swerved around the sheep – I stayed well hidden, not to be seen. Many were returning again, like Valerie in her cheerful-looking camper van; she turned off the valley road and twisted up the track towards Tups Tump in search of a quiet spot.

Valerie parked by an old stone stile near a stream, beyond was a pathway meandering up the hillside; she got out, slamming the door, and gazed in wonder at the meadows of wild flowers. Breathing in deeply, Valerie was pleased to be back in my Lovely Valley where the air was pure and clean. She slid open the van's side door and took out a big shoulder bag, a basket of food and a paint-splattered wooden frame with a flat board attached to it. Bobbin and Clover watched this curious sight from afar.

After following the pathway up the hill, Valerie found a level area to spread a blanket and set out her picnic food. She propped up the frame and opened a box with tubes of colours and bristly brushes.

Peering up the mountain, Valerie scribbled lines over the board until she smiled, happy with her marks. She delved into the box for some tubes and from them squeezed bright dollops on to a plate. Then dabbing with a long brush, she delighted in sweeping those lush colours over her board.

Hiding behind a plump resting sheep, Bobbin declared to Clover that he had never seen anything the like that magical board. Valerie completed her painting, stirred her brush into a cup of water and sat back feeling pleased with her creation – then she noticed on the hillside something missing from her picture. Squinting her eyes Valerie could see a row of leafy spikes peeking over the heather; just like foxgloves, but she was sure they weren't there earlier. Baffled by their unexpected appearance Valerie decided to fetch her spyglasses from her camper van to have a closer look.

Meanwhile, those leafy spikes began to bob down the hillside until I could see that they were certainly not foxgloves but the ears of a rabble of large rabbits. Bobbin and Clover watched anxiously as the unknown rabbits advanced towards Valerie's healthy picnic with their noses a-twitching.

Valerie returned up the pathway, clasping her spyglasses, keen to solve the puzzling sight. As she arrived over the bank she couldn't believe it, what a proper mess. That rabble of hungry rabbits was raiding her picnic – chewing on carrot and lettuce salad. Others had breadcrumbs clinging to their whiskers; one was even trying to lick the pattern off her flowery plate.

"Shoo, Shoo," puffed Valerie and the raiding rabbits fled back up the hill. Bobbin turned to Clover and whispered, "We must follow the rabbits and stop them invading our valley, they mustn't mix with us – it's bad luck."

The two rabbits scampered up a dark rabbit hole until they surfaced into bright sunshine at the top of Tups Tump. Bobbin could see the big rabbits grouped together and he told Clover to stay in the hole until he returned.

Bobbin crept behind a hawthorn tree and could hear them chattering. "We'll try again, as soon as the others get here," said the biggest rabbit.

"They can't be far," agreed another, who still had lettuce dangling from his mouth. Bobbin was troubled, fearing these unwelcome rabbits would overrun the valley and he bravely stepped out to face the rabble.

"What are you doing in our valley?" demanded Bobbin in his crossest voice. The rebel rabbits nervously stood up tall surprised at seeing Bobbin.

"I am Ronald," said the biggest rabbit, "we fled our burrows to escape the Metal Monsters who are attacking our land."

Bobbin listened carefully, "Would that be in Distant Lands?" he asked.

"Yes, many Metal Monsters with huge claws are cutting a great tunnel towards our homes," continued Ronald, "Billowing out awful smells as they rip up our land and growling their strange grunts – we were so afraid."

– I thought that explained the weird noises echoing down my Lovely Valley.

Over the mountain appeared more rabbits from Distant Lands, many with their Little Ones bouncing behind. They greeted each other by rubbing noses and Bobbin carefully considered what he should do next.

Clover crept up to Bobbin wanting to join the group and his father placed his paw on his shoulder. Once the rabbits had calmed down, Bobbin explained to them that stranger-rabbits were not allowed into the valley. "We mustn't mix, it brings bad luck," he told them.

"But we need to live somewhere else," begged Ronald, and the others appealed to Bobbin to let them stay. What a problem Bobbin had – but before he had time to respond a huge shadow unexpectedly slid over the mountain as clouds blew into the valley bringing big drops of rain.

"Quick, over here!" shouted Bobbin and he led them to an old barn on the side of the hill – rabbits hate wet weather. They followed him into the cosy space through a split in the big barn doors. The old stone barn was stacked with bales of 'summer-smelling' hay, many piled up to the top. A family of mice emerged from between the bales but quickly dashed back in again, as rabbits didn't usually visit.

The rain hammered on the roof and water dribbled in where slates had slipped but the new colony of rabbits was glad to be safely together.

Bobbin felt he and Clover must hurry back home, the other rabbits agreed to live in the barn until he returned. So the two rabbits ventured out into the cold rain and they cringed as it poured down really hard on them – Bobbin wondered if this was the start of bad luck?

Valerie was still clearing up her scattered lunch when the storm approached. In a panic she gathered up the corners of her picnic blanket, clattering the crockery inside as she crammed it into her basket. Grabbing her shoulder bag, Valerie turned to rescue her 'work of colours' but found to her horror it was now dribbling from the heavy raindrops. Annoyed by her spoilt picture she left it there, fearing 'fern green' would be dripping over everything in her neat little van, and decided to collect it later. Dashing down the hill and into the shelter of her camper van, Valerie brewed up a pot of tea, dried off and sat to watch the rain as it clattered loudly on the metal roof.

The skies began to rumble as clouds crashed together, Bobbin and Clover ran off home. They found some old rabbit holes, but could not use them as they were flowing with water – just like drainpipes. So continuing over land they jumped the rising springs and tracked around large puddles until they were faced with a mire of thick sticky mud. Sheep in that boggy field were up to their knees in sludge as they struggled to move in their heavy wet coats. The rabbits slipped along the raised verge of the hedgerow and were relieved to arrive back home at Golden Glade to tell of their troubling tale.

The rabbits gathered around the wet twosome as they flopped down exhausted from their journey. Bobbin told them about the runaway rabbits and the menacing Metal Monsters attacking their burrows in Distant Lands.

The day darkened as the storm turned really nasty; it circled about like a caged beast, trapped between the valley's high mountains. Thunder crashed as water poured down the hillsides ignoring all normal routes, instead finding paths and farm tracks to flow along.

The weather was creating havoc in the valley; even I couldn't blow those angry clouds away. Sheep ran for their lives when a great landslide oozed down the mountainside near the Crooked Village, carrying trees and stony walls in its mass of squishy soil. Waterlogged trees tipped over when their roots could no longer grip the riverbanks.

A stash of branches drifted down a stream until it jammed in the shallow ford behind Tumble Towers. The water diverted down the meadow and flooded the lawn of the Tower Inn where the lights sparkled on the silent, rising water. Inside, patrons munched and sipped unaware of the lake forming outside the Inn – until it spilled in under the bar door.

Customers ceased their chatter as water trickled down the steps into the bar – but being a curious lot, the door was opened allowing in a great tidal wave as the wayward stream cascaded in.

"Don't panic," reassured the barman, "it's 'appened before, 'twill go down storeroom drain." Sure enough the water flowed under the counter and through to the back, as the locals lifted their feet and continued drinking.

Valerie curled up in bed with her hot water bottle, she hadn't expected this sort of weather and was feeling quite cold but she soon fell into a deep sleep despite the blustery weather rocking her little camper van.

The storm continued all night, ditches alongside the lanes failed to cope and spilt over, stones and brown water bubbled from gateways, turning the valley road into a river. A convoy of frogs marched along, joyfully splashing about with their clumsy webbed feet loving the spell of wet weather.

Metal motors attempted to leave my Lovely Valley ploughing through the muddy current; its depth had caused some to splutter and choke, then cease to move. One abandoned little white motor was found gliding about on the water like a stray swan. As the torrents swelled, unbeknown to Valerie, her van started to float and drift off gently down the winding track.

Harry Salmon stretched his tail in the rising river and swam about delighted with the idea of being able to return home soon. He wriggled from side to side flexing his body, enjoying the rush of water through his gills and blew out a trail of big bubbles. As he prepared for his journey home he noticed a strange shadow pass over him, cruising down the river was a four-wheeled vessel — just like a camper van. Inside, still asleep, was Valerie. She dreamt of sailing on the ocean, aboard an old galleon ship, until it swayed so roughly that she awoke, realising something was very wrong.

The rabbits of Golden Glade Warren rose to find the valley river had overflowed into the glade and had completely surrounded them. A huddle of muddy sheep sheltered at the top of their little hill. Bobbin took control and called all the rabbits out of their burrows. "We haven't got long before the water will flood our homes," he said anxiously, "and we need to get off our hillock before we are stranded!"

"But our Little Ones can't jump the water," declared another rabbit. "We need a bridge," suggested Flora, and they began to look about until they found an old fallen branch. They pushed hard until it rolled down the hill and fell just in the right place spanning the water. The rabbits swiftly hopped safely along the log just before the rushing water shifted it a little. "Where's my Little Ones?" cried Flora, then she spied them still at the opening of their burrow. Cuddling together, Clover, Bramble, Snowy and Lily watched wide-eyed with terror, having never seen the likes of such a deluge. "Quick, my lovelies!" insisted Flora, "Before it's too late!"

Nervous of the big smelly sheep around them, Clover edged his way out and the others followed him down to the water. Staying close together they carefully balanced on the log bridge and shuffled slowly along. Suddenly the log shifted and broke loose from the banks, casting away in the rush of the current, while the poor little bunnies clung on for their dear lives.

Desperate to save their babies, Bobbin and Flora ran along the bank after them, but the log flowed off towards the bubbling rapids of the Valley River and they were swept away. Disappearing out of sight they listened as their bunnies cried out, until the roar of the river drowned their calls.

Bobbin and Flora could not go any further, the muds and floods were all about them and they just didn't know what to do next.

Clover, Bramble, Snowy and Lily held tightly as the log wobbled and pitched in the fast-moving water, their short lives flashed before them. Clover regretted not seeing Distant Lands, Bramble thought he would never taste the bramble's berries and Snowy wouldn't even get to play in the snow. Lily remembered meeting Harry the big friendly fish in Millydill Pool.

Cattle balanced on earthy mounds, looking caringly at the doomed bunnies as they rushed past. Twigs spun violently in the river, while a frightened fox perched on a fencepost and considered his fate. Small creatures clung to thorny bushes to escape the waterlogged land.

A fleet of yellow plastic ducks bobbed by in complete confusion, now afloat after years of capture in tangled roots and rocky regions, following the valley 'Back a Quack' events. However, the strangest sight of all was the colourful camper van sailing along, with Valerie's anxious face pressing against the misted-up window, as disaster fell upon my Lovely Valley.

Near the Crooked Village gathered an audience of humble-beings peering over the edge of the old bridge. They discussed whether it would stand the force of the river thrashing against the narrow archway.

Then folk exchanged their flooding reports – all having a tale to tell.

Mrs Jones told of last night – her and Mr Jones were watching the picture box when they be hearing clinking noises.

"Thought it were Merlin the cat disturbing things in the cellar," and she added tunefully, "later we went to look, water was upta fourth step with bottles of elderberry merrily floating about!"

Bill, The Mill, found his old hen house missing. "Ad foxy stolen the lot?" he laughed, "found it drifting about in bo'um field, 'ens were still sitting on eggs, ha ha."

"I pulled out a fair few motors this morning," mumbled Sam, "spect 'ere be more 'fore days done," and there was his tractor ready for action.

Cherry at Chapel Cottage had a home full of damp folk who were marooned for the night. "Muddy footprints everywhere," she moaned.

The boy Lewis had with him his big dog Larry the lurcher. "Larry 'ates wet weather, ha'to drag him out," and he declared, "NESH!" all grownupily – expect that was his Grandma's word. Larry looked abashed as they laughed at him and he feared his 'top dog' image had been cruelly crushed.

Redeeming his cleverness Larry the Lurcher's ears stood straight up as he fixed his gaze down river. All eyes turned and strained to see through the overhanging branches – just what was floating towards them?

"It's a camper van," exclaimed Bill. The local folk fled off the bridge as the van crashed and wedged itself in the arch. Valerie screamed for help and tapped like mad on the van window. "Get me out of here!" she yelled.

Sam stepped into action, organising his towrope and positioning his tractor.

"My word," said Cherry, "whatever next," and she pointed towards the bunnies sailing along on their log. Everyone gasped as the log hit Valerie's camper van trapping the bunnies in a torrent of bubbling river. Larry tried leaping into the river to chase those furry ones, forgetting he didn't like water, but Lewis hung on tightly to his collar. The bunnies shook with fear as the log rocked about, knowing they couldn't hold on for much longer. Then Lily caught sight of a large fishy fin – it was her friend Harry Salmon.

"Look at that huge fish," declared Bill, as Harry's big tail gently began to push the log towards the bank. Clover, Bramble, Snowy and Lily made the biggest hops ever landing safely onto grassy land. Lily looked back to see Harry waving his tail goodbye as he dived deep under the camper van.

She called out, "Swim away Harry!" and he began his long journey home.

"Wish I'ad me gun," whinged Mr Jones. "Wish I'ad me net," replied Bill.

The bunnies fled up the fields and hid under a thorny thicket. Panting with exhaustion, Bramble puffed, "That was a near one." Once they had calmed down they curled up together and fell asleep.

Flora and Bobbin returned home cold and weary, after a long night searching for their bunnies. At Golden Glade the rabbits were desperately trying to build up a barrier to prevent the water from flooding their burrows – the place looked like a disaster area with broken daffodils and scattered driftwood. The rabbits were caked in mud from ears to tail and when Flora and Bobbin arrived they could hardly recognise them.

"We failed to save our dear Little Ones," cried Flora sadly, not knowing their fate, and the other rabbits gathered around to comfort them.

"They're most likely be far away in Other Lands by now," said one blundering rabbit causing Flora to cry even more and the others tutted in disapproval at his clumsy remark.

"Come on!" called one tired rabbit, "let's keep working, or we will lose our homes as well." They turned their efforts to keeping the muddy wall standing as all the rabbits joined in digging, heaping and patting the wet earth.  But the water kept seeping over until eventually they were forced to jump onto high ground and watch in horror as the wall collapsed and water flooded into Golden Glade Warren. "It's hopeless," cried the rabbits.

Clover woke first and wondered where he was, then remembered their scary journey down the river. Carefully he looked out from the thicket to check if it was safe and then nudged the others to wake up. The rain had eased a little and they quietly tipped-toed out to have a nibble of grass — unaware that they were being spied on from high up on the mountain.

The bunnies had never been away from their warren before and were becoming scared and confused not knowing which way to set off home.

"Let's go to the top of the hill," suggested Lily, "we might see Golden Glade from there." So dodging the brooks and slippery muds they reached a rocky outcrop overlooking the valley; they were amazed at the flooded fields spreading for acres around the course of the river. Many sheep gathered on grassy mounds while tractors attempted to reach them. The bunnies could not see Golden Glade, there were so many trees hiding the land and feared they would never see home again.

Clover felt uneasy, he sensed something about and feared they were being hunted down. He sniffed the air and could smell a strong musty stench. He squeaked to the others, "let's get out of here," — but it was too late. A stinky fox stood there staring at them little bunnies as they froze with panic. Foxy smiled wickedly with his sharp teeth glistening while dribble trickled down from his mean mouth — hungry for his breakfast.

The terrified bunnies were ready to fight for their lives; Bramble clenched his furry fists and bounced about punching the air like a march hare. Foxy knew they hadn't a chance of survival against a crafty fox like him but he enjoyed watching him. He swished his huge red tail in delight, but soon he became bored – as Foxy preferred fast food. He was about to snarl at the bunnies so he could chase and catch them when Ronald bounded between them and pulled a most frightening face at Foxy. Foxy recoiled with surprise – he had never seen such a big and ugly rabbit – and decided he wasn't hungry any more so turned tail and ran away.

The little bunnies were still shaking as Clover explained that Ronald was one of the friendly runaway rabbits and they thanked him for saving them.

"What are you doing up here alone?" questioned Ronald.

"We were swept away in the floods, but we were able to escape," answered Clover, thinking that his new lucky name must have worked.

Then they followed Ronald up the valley to the big landslide of earth.

"Wow," gasped Snowy, "that would make a great playground," and he imagined chasing about in a maze of burrows. Ronald led them along his earlier paw tracks, then further on until they could see the barn where the new rabbits were living. Clover remembered passing that way with his father and declared excitedly that he knew the way home.

Hopping along in a line, Clover, Bramble, Snowy, Lily with Ronald following, made their way down the mountain. Wading across fields of boggy mud, they slid under a hedgerow into the meadow passing Valerie's magical board – but it was showing nothing today. Slipping along the verge of the waterlogged field and squeezing between the fencing wires, the bunnies laughed at Ronald as he strained to push his big tummy through. After jumping onto islands of rocks, they smelt the familiar homely scent of their warren and soon could see the daffodils leading to Golden Glade.

The bunnies called out as they neared their warren, Flora's ears twitched as her heart skipped a beat, was it really her Little Ones – or just the strange sounds of the rushing waters?

Flora turned to see all of her Little Ones racing towards her; she was so thrilled to see them and hugged them all very tightly. The other rabbits had been watching helplessly as the water rose dangerously up to their burrows. They all rushed over to join the excitement, amazed to see that the bunnies had safely survived their fateful voyage down the river and were keen to hear about their adventures.

Ronald inspected the state of Golden Glade Warren, the water was now lapping by the entrance to their homes, he told the others not to give up as he would be back soon and he scampered off up the mountain.

The rabbits cuddled up under the shelter of a bush and the four Little Ones told of their daunting time and how Harry the stray fish had saved them. Lily hoped Harry Salmon had found his way home too.

Bobbin thought it was time to tell of a tale that had been passed down the families of Golden Glade and the rabbits listened with interest.

"A long, long time ago, the original rabbits of our warren once lived the other side of Fforest Mountain – at Rocky Warren by the waterfalls in Steeply Valley. Set on the sunny side, they shared the land with tatty sheep that grazed the hillside. A pretty church sat below amongst a village of small cottages where humble-beings wandered to and fro. Then one day countless other-beings marched into the village and changed valley life. Soon the locals left." Bobbin scratched his nose and continued.

"Noisy work went on and wooden homes appeared, then came a great wall that stretched from hillside to hillside. Our rabbits moved further along the valley to a quieter spot, but one day the stream began to fill up and water crept back up the valley. The great wall had blocked the stream causing a giant lake, it drowned the village along with their new burrows – so the legend is happening again," he said sadly. "What happened next?" asked Clover. Bobbin explained, "The rabbits of Rocky Warren ventured over Mountain Fforest until they found this peaceful setting in Golden Glade.

4-20 The Drowned Valley

"Here we are!" shouted Ronald as his rabble splashed through the water around Golden Glade, "Get to work," he ordered his lot.

The rabbits of Golden Glade hopped out from under the bush to see the runaway rabbits digging, shifting and piling up clumps of mud with their big strong paws. Stones were placed into the barrier as they struggled against the overflowing river. Working unceasingly, slipping about in the sticky mire, the exhausted rabbits fought hard to secure the wall, until at last the river no longer spilled into their Glade.

The Little Ones jumped about with glee as the runaway rabbits collapsed with tiredness among the broken clumps of daffodils, but the job was done and Golden Glade Warren had been saved.

Bobbin and the other rabbits were so pleased to have their homes back and thanked the runaway rabbits for their efforts. They agreed that they had not brought bad luck but instead spared them from disaster. They fussed around the muddy gang and Bobbin invited them to live in the valley. Ronald was grateful for the offer and decided they would live in the old barn until drier weather made it better for digging a new warren. Snowy suggested that the landslide could be the perfect place for a home, Ronald smiled at him. The runaway rabbits cleaned themselves in a big puddle and made their way back up the hill to the old barn.

After a time the weather calmed and the sun beamed down between the grey parting clouds that were still sprinkling the last of their showers. The rabbits slowly appeared from their burrows, they were pleased to feel the heat of the sun and see the ground was drying well.

The barrier worked, the river had now dropped to a sensible level and the flooding was gone. The daffodils lifted their heads and were standing upright again while little creatures appeared from tangled nooks to nibble and be happy with life.

Bobbin turned to Flora, "Let's take the family up to see the runaway rabbits," and they rounded up Clover, Bramble, Snowy and Lily and headed for the old barn on the hill.

The sheep were back in their meadows and Bobbin hoped the farmer hadn't seen the runaway rabbits in his old barn. They hurried along until they saw Valerie's magical board still positioned in the meadow and the Little Ones hopped over to it. Clover told of the tasty colours he saw and touched the white board with his muddy paw. Lily, seeing his print had marked the board, put her own paws on too. Excitedly, they all joined in until there was a crazy paw print picture. Bobbin called them away, he had found the rabbit hole that led up to the top, so they followed him along the tunnel – still giggling at the mess they had created.

On the top the runaway rabbits were grazing nearby, they looked up to see the family and Ronald scampered over, saying cheerfully, "A fine day for a wander," and they were pleased to see him.

Clover pestered Ronald, "Will you show us where you came from?"

"Not so fast, Clover," Flora said firmly, "expect Ronald has more important things to do." She was thinking he wouldn't like to see those Metal Monsters digging up his warren – but Ronald politely answered. "Yes, let us go and see," and he called all of his rabbits to come too.

Racing through the bracken to the top of the mountain the rabbits could see the flat endless view of Distant Lands. Ronald remembered the destruction they had left behind and was prepared for a sorrowful sight – but there was not a Monster to be seen. The patchwork fields were neat and tidy, only an earthy line passing by. The runaway rabbits cheered excitedly when they could see their warren was still there. "We can go home!" A beautiful arch of colours appeared in the sky, spanning gracefully over Distant Lands. Clover was amazed. "What is that?" he asked curiously. Bobbin smiled, "It's a rainbow, my son, and it means, all will be well."

Later they rubbed noses goodbye, as the runaway rabbits were keen to return home, "Come and see us soon!" called Bobbin and they watched their white tails bob along disappearing down the mountain.

So that was that – the rabbits mixed after years of fearing outsiders, but as it happened both colonies were able to help each other in their own unique way. They agreed to meet up every spring on the mountain – that's if the weather was not wet.

The fields dried out nicely producing the lushest spread of grass ever seen and the rabbits of Golden Glade thrived on it. When the landslide had turned green the Little Ones called it Slippylands and they did build that maze of tunnels to play in. Foxy never dared to bother them again.

Valerie's camper van was towed from the river and after a few days it chugged back into life again. She returned to collect her magical board only to find the rabbits' splendid muddy 'paw print' picture – I too did include my dragony foot, however it was a little large. Well I thought Valerie might need some cheering up. She hung it above her fireplace at home and spent many an evening studying it. Valerie did return plenty of times to my Lovely Valley and created lots of her colourful images and even sold a few.

Harry Salmon found his way home, he told all his friends about his fishy adventures and becoming stranded in our beautiful valley.

No real harm was done in all that bad weather and valley life continued normally – as if it is ever normal here?

.....................there's lovely.

## Proper Dragon Tales

DVD – 'Do you Believe in Dragons?' A charming short fantasy film about Caroline Downey as a child discovering the Proper Dragon and later remembering the stories he told her. Featuring local scenes in the Llanthony Valley. Also includes 'Step into my pages' presented by Caroline explaining her painting techniques and how the Proper Dragon Tales books are created. – See website for full details.

## Next Book No. 5 The Forgotten Farm
Published Sept. 10

'The Forgotten Farm' was a distant memory to William when he received the news that he had inherited his uncle's home in the valley. The decision to move with his family caused a big change in their lifestyle, farming work was not easy and problems threatened the future of the old farmhouse.

# Proper Dragon Tales

## How to order Books and Prints

You may order directly from Caroline Downey
or via the Website.  www.properdragontales.co.uk
Framed Canvas Prints are available from images in this book.
Please quote titles and code numbers when ordering.

No.1 'The Black Mountain Sheep' is an enchanting story of strange happenings after the sheep were removed from the mountainside at the time of the Foot and Mouth crisis.  However it is a tale of hope and regeneration told with lively dialogue by the Proper Dragon who exists in his lovely valley. Published Sept. 06

No.2 'Shadows in the Fforest' follows the capers of Larry long-legs the naughty lurcher dog when he disrupts the peacefulness of the valley.  But he has a plan to put things right and he ventures with Pickles the trekking pony into the woods where peculiar and wonderful events send them deeper into the forest.  Published Sept. 07

No.3 'Secret of the Standing Stones' is revealed to Gwillim the greedy Billy Goat who suffers the consequences of eating a scrap too many when scarecrow and canvas tent seemed to be his preferred feast.  His adventure into the sacred circle of ancient rocks presents a challenging time for Gwillim. Published Sept. 08